ABOUT THE ALDEN ALL STARS

Nothing's more important to Nick, Sam, Justin, and Dennis than their team, the Alden Panthers. Whether the sport is football, basketball, baseball, or soccer, the four seventh-graders can always be found practicing, sweating, and giving their all. Sometimes the Panthers are on their way to a winning season, and sometimes the team can't do anything right. But no matter what, you can be sure the ALDEN ALL STARS are playing to win.

Chock-full of plays, sports details, and plenty of exciting sports action, the ALDEN ALL STARS series is just right for anyone who loves to compete—or just loves a good story.

# Jester in the Backcourt

**ALDEN ALL STARS**

# Jester in the Backcourt

## Tommy Hallowell

PUFFIN BOOKS

PUFFIN BOOKS
Published by the Penguin Group
Viking Penguin, a division of Penguin Books USA Inc.,
40 West 23rd Street, New York, New York 10010, U.S.A.
Penguin Books Ltd, 27 Wrights Lane, London W8 5TZ, England
Penguin Books Australia Ltd, Ringwood, Victoria, Australia
Penguin Books Canada Ltd, 2801 John Street, Markham, Ontario, Canada L3R 1B4
Penguin Books (N.Z.) Ltd, 182–190 Wairau Road, Auckland 10, New Zealand

Penguin Books Ltd, Registered Offices: Harmondsworth, Middlesex, England

First published in Puffin Books 1990
1  3  5  7  9  10  8  6  4  2
Copyright © Daniel Weiss and Associates, 1990
All rights reserved

LIBRARY OF CONGRESS CATALOGING IN PUBLICATION DATA
Hallowell, Tommy.    Jester in the back court / Tommy Hallowell.    p.    cm.
Summary: Nick has to learn to control his antics on the basketball
court if the Alden Panthers are going to win the championship.
ISBN 0-14-032911-0
[1. Basketball—Fiction.]  I. Title.
PZ7.H164Je  1990    [Fic]—dc20    89-10919

Printed in the United States of America
Set in Century Schoolbook

*To Dylan Kelley, who was so good.*

# Jester in the Backcourt

# 1

"Banzai!!"

The wild, heart-stopping shriek rose above the thumping sound of basketballs bouncing against the gym's hardwood floor. Alden Junior High School's seventh-grade basketball team was shooting around before practice. Nick Wilkerson had just flung up a crazy half-court shot and let loose his special war whoop to go with it.

All his teammates turned at the scream and watched as the ball floated through the air. Nick was a good shot. They were waiting for the day he made one of these "banzai" shots. Today wasn't the day. The ball passed ten feet over the backboard and then jammed itself between two metal poles that were part of the rigging. Sometimes shots got stuck between the hoop and the backboard, but no one had ever seen a ball get stuck so far up. Everyone laughed and hooted. Sam McCaskill started to throw another ball at it to knock it loose.

"Wait, Sam," Nick said, holding his arm. "Don't hit it. I think it might still go in."

"Let go of my arm, Mr. Banzai. That shot came closer to going into outer space than going in the basket."

Sam threw the ball and hit one pole, but didn't loosen Nick's ball. Two other guys tried and missed. Sam's second shot was a direct hit, and the two balls came down together.

As Sam caught one, Nick snuck up behind him and whipped Sam's shorts down, then knocked the ball away and dribbled to the other end of the court.

"Oh, grow up," Sam griped, pulling his shorts back up.

"Never!" Nick yelled. As he approached the other basket, Dennis Clements came out to guard him. Nick shimmied left and right, dribbled behind his back, then bounced the ball through Dennis's legs, picked it up on the other side, and put in the lay-up.

"Major league burn!" Nick yelled, jumping on Dennis's back. "Hi ho, Silver, away!"

Laughing, Dennis gave Nick a piggyback ride down the court while Nick dribbled with his free hand.

Nick was the team clown, and he looked the part. His straight, dirty-blond hair was indented across the back by the rubber band that held his glasses securely to his head. He wore long boxer shorts which hung three inches below his gym shorts, and instead of white socks, he wore gray hunting socks with Day-Glo orange stripes.

When Coach Gimigliano came into the gym and called the players together, Nick, Sam, Dennis, and Justin Johnson sat together in the bleachers. The four were the best of friends, and had been ever since their years together at Fairwood Elementary.

This year the foursome had moved up to Alden Junior High. They had all played on the seventh-grade football team in the fall, and even though the season hadn't gone too well for the Panthers, they had had a great time. When December rolled around, they had all gone out for basketball. Only Justin hadn't made the final cut. It was a disappointment, but not a surprise. Of the four, Justin had played the least on the football squad. His small size was often a disadvantage. Soccer was his favorite sport, but Alden didn't have a team.

Despite not making the basketball team, Justin had figured a way to stick with the Panthers. He had convinced Coach Gimigliano to make him team manager. He took care of the balls and game jerseys, and during practice he helped keep the players on their toes. Justin couldn't dribble straight, but he knew plenty about plays and strategies.

So the foursome was together after all.

"Okay, guys," Coach said. "I've got to take care of some business for ten minutes. Justin will run you through some of those lay-up drills we did yesterday." He left the gym.

"Um, you guys remember the drill?" Justin asked.

"No, teach us!" Nick said, laughing.

"All right, all right, just go do it," Justin replied. The players climbed down and organized themselves into a simple lay-up drill.

Nick took his turn, threw a head fake and dropped in a reverse lay-up.

"Hot dog," Dennis said.

"Hey, if you've got it flaunt it," Nick said. Instead of getting back in line, he joined Justin on the bench.

"What are you doing, 'Coach'?"

"Nothing. Get back on the court," Justin said, as he continued to write out the names of the players on a chart.

"Can't," Nick said. "I have a, uh, twisted ankle. Yeah, that's it, a twisted ankle. Do you want me to describe each player for your notes?"

"Do I have a choice?"

"No. Now shooting—and missing—is Pockets O'Brien," Nick began, talking loudly enough so every player could hear him. "At five-foot-ten, Pockets is the tallest player by a head. He has been named the starting center despite an almost total lack of talent. He also has the weirdest nickname."

As each player took his turn, Nick went into his sportscaster voice.

"Speaking of weird nicknames, here comes the second weirdest—Mugsy Neilson.

"Now up, Dennis Clements, the starting forward, who was also named team captain even though no one likes him.

"Jeremy Blake—the human cannonball!

"Alex Kratchman—not bad considering he is completely blind.

"Another starter, Paul Sacks. He bribed Coach G. for his starting guard position.

"And here's Kevin McEnroe, guard. Wow, he made a lay-up! *That's* a surprise.

"Next up, Sam McCaskill, great quarterback, terrible forward. Stick to football!"

"Oh, shut up!" Sam said as he ran by.

"Hey, this is constructive criticism, that's all."

"Don't you ever stop talking, Wilkerson?" Coach Gimigliano asked. Nick hadn't noticed his return. He smiled sheepishly and jogged back into the lay-up line.

Along with Pockets, Dennis, and Paul, the other starters were Nick at guard, and Kyle Bushmiller at forward. With fourteen players on the squad, Coach had promised that everyone would get into the games. Tomorrow they would open the season by playing North Colby Junior High.

Nick was ready for the game. He had been a force in their practice games—his main problem was letting his attention wander while Coach went over the basics for the other guys. *His* only worry was that the rest of the team wasn't ready. This was the last practice before the opener and his teammates were still having trouble getting down the defensive and offensive positions. Coach G. had given them a couple of plays to run, but every time he introduced something new, their fundamentals—dribbling, passing—would fall apart. They would be thinking too much and would forget the basics. It almost seemed like they had gotten worse in the preseason practices.

Worst of all, Nick's jokes about their starting center, Pockets O'Brien, weren't far from true. As tall as he was, Pockets had the potential to be a valuable, even dominant player under the basket, but right now he couldn't shoot, pass, or dribble. Even his rebounding, which should have been natural, needed work. In fact, Nick wondered whether Coach G. was making a good decision by starting Pockets.

One guy Nick wasn't worried about was himself. Hoop was his sport. He had always been the best shooter in the neighborhood and he handled the ball well. Early in practice, Coach tried to discourage Nick from dribbling between his legs and behind his back, but he soon saw that Nick could do those things *and* stay in full control. He was made the point guard, the man who started the offense, bringing the ball upcourt.

Nick was psyched that the season was starting. He was confident that he would do his share of scoring against North Colby.

But he also wanted to win.

# 2

Nick brought the ball up and was met by the opposing guard at half-court. He passed to Dennis, spun past his man and took the return pass at the top of the key. Wide open, he put up a jump shot. It was a foot and a half short, missing completely. He heard a few cries of "air ball" from the North Colby bleachers. North rebounded.

He muttered to himself.

"Don't worry about it," Dennis said.

Unfortunately, it was typical of the game so far.

Watching the boys from Alden play their season opener, no one would have guessed that the object of basketball was to put the orange ball through the round hoop. No one could score. Dribblers bounced balls off their own feet; passers seemed to prefer the opposing team's players; and the shooters, apparently, had stayed at home.

Luckily for the toothless Panthers, the North Colby team was playing just as terribly as they were, matching them misstep for misstep. Five minutes had ticked away—half of the first quarter—before someone finally scored. It was Kyle Bushmiller, Alden's forward, who woke up the scorekeeper. He missed two short jumpers, each time collecting his own rebound, before he finally hit. Still, it counted, and Alden took the lead.

After his own first crummy shot, Nick was reluctant to try again. All his preseason confidence disappeared. This was the real thing—and a disaster. With two minutes left in the first, leading 6–4, Coach Gimigliano put in the first round of substitutes. Zack Shapiro came in for Nick, who sat down next to Sam.

"So what's the problem out there?" Sam asked, handing Nick a towel to dry his sweaty hands and face.

Nick seemed to think it over carefully while catching his breath.

"No cheerleaders," he said finally, with a straight face.

"What?" Sam said, laughing.

"No cheerleaders. Do you see even *one* cheerleader out on the sideline? No. Now if we had cheerleaders, well then you'd see some basketball. We'd play two hundred percent better, guaranteed."

Sam and some others on the bench laughed halfheartedly.

"Come to think of it," Nick added, "if we let cheerleaders *play* for the team, we'd probably do two hundred percent better."

That got a big laugh, and Coach, who hadn't heard any of the conversation, looked over at them with a puzzled expression. Nick looked out at the court innocently, as though he didn't know what all the giggling was about. He was getting the feeling Coach wasn't a big fan of wisecracking.

By halftime the play had picked up a little, but baskets were still hard to come by. North now led by a point, 13–12. Nick had tried only one more shot in the first half and missed it. During halftime he resolved not to be so gun-shy.

Nick's new resolve paid off quickly as he sank a

fifteen-footer to chalk up the first bucket of the second half. North missed, and Alden took possession. The ball came to Nick again and he went up, but then passed inside to Sam, who laid the ball up and in. A minute later Nick sank another jumper and Alden was soon riding a five-point lead.

The fourth quarter was a disaster. Though Alden kept ahead by four points or so, the level of play dropped back down. No one could hold on to the ball.

Dennis fed Pockets in the low post. Pockets pivoted left, looked, and then pivoted on the other foot. The whistle blew.

"Travel!" the referee barked, making the signal.

North passed the ball inbounds. Paul stepped in and stripped the ball, but then passed it to Nick in the backcourt. The whistle blew again.

"Over and back!"

For the next ten minutes the hardest-working person on the floor was the referee, who was busy calling all the violations: reaching in, double dribbles, even triple dribbles!

Coach G. would start to yell from the sideline, but would shake his head instead. It confirmed Nick's worst fears. Everything the Panthers had practiced was forgotten. Pockets was a total loss. He looked like he was playing volleyball under the basket. With his height he was getting his hands on every rebound, but wasn't holding on to any of them. It was embarrassing.

On the plus side Nick sank another jumper and Dennis added two fast-break baskets. That, plus a few free throws, was it. Luckily, North's offensive performance was even worse, and Alden started the season with a win, 24–20.

Nick finished the game with six points. Only Dennis had more, with seven. So despite the team bumbling—and his own missed shots and crummy passes—Nick felt all right about his performance that night. It was the first game, after all, and at least they had won.

At Thursday's practice Coach G. congratulated them on their win, but then took them straight back to square one. Instead of running the trapping and screening plays he had introduced last week, he put everyone through long, exhausting hours of dribbling practice, passing practice, and lay-up drills.

"Is Coach trying to kill us?" Pockets whispered to Nick during a rare break in the action. He bent forward to catch his breath.

"This isn't punishment," Coach said before Nick could reply. "This is what we need to work on."

12

Nick agreed with Coach, but felt that he was ready to move on. This simple stuff was fine for guys like Pockets. For him, it was boring. He was desperate to liven things up, and so took a few long-range shots with the "banzai" war whoop. He didn't make any, but he did win three baseball cards from Max by hitting the rim from half-court plus.

When Nick missed a lay-up he crossed his elbows and stumbled knock-kneed back into line. The next time through he tried, unsuccessfully, to lay it up behind his back.

"Watch this next one," Nick said to Dennis. "It's my patented slamma-wamma-jamma slam dunk."

"Right," Dennis said. "A slam dunk?"

Nick took the pass, leapt toward the hoop and "dunked" the ball *upward* through the hoop. He then did a victory dance that looked like a cross between break-dancing and having a fit. The other players laughed.

The more laughs he got, the more Nick did whatever he could to be funny, even with Coach watching.

Coach G. took Nick's shenanigans in stride. When he wasn't goofing around, Nick worked hard—and played well. So Coach was patient, even when all the fun slowed down practice.

When Nick tried to drop-kick a pass during some

13

lay-ups, he accidentally knocked the ball way off the court. Justin retrieved it.

"Knock it off," Justin said, tossing the ball back to Nick. "You're messing up the drill."

"Excuse me," Nick replied. "Coach G. will tell me if it's a problem."

"It's no big deal, I'm just saying . . ."

"I'm a natural-born entertainer, Justin, that's all."

"Fine, forget I said anything."

Friday's practice was more of the same and when Coach Gimigliano left the gym, Nick took center stage, inventing his "Bad Globetrotter" routine. Nick started out pretending to do some of the trick passes and dribbling they had all seen the Harlem Globetrotters perform, but of course he couldn't. So instead he made the tricks worse and worse.

Whistling "Sweet Georgia Brown"—the Globetrotters' theme song—Nick twisted the ball back and forth in one hand as if it were spinning. Then he tried rolling the ball across his shoulders but bounced it off the side of his head. Then he went to the low, fast dribble—but with the ball just sitting on the floor. Suddenly he noticed that the laughter had faded.

Nick looked up. His whistling slowed down and then stopped. He smiled innocently at Coach G.

"All right, Wilkerson," Coach said sternly. "That's enough for one day. The song-and-dance won't help us beat Williamsport tomorrow. Got it?"

Nick nodded, blushing. Coach had never come down on him before. *Geez, I'm just trying to have a little fun,* he thought.

# 3

"So I'm taking the ball to the hoop and I'm floating in the air, oh, eight maybe ten feet in the air," Nick was saying.

"C'mon," Justin said. "Tell me what really happened."

Justin had missed Saturday's game against Williamsport because of a family trip, so the others were filling him in on the details over lunch on Monday. Alden had won easily, 31–24. They had all done well, but Nick was stretching the facts.

"All right, maybe six feet high. . . . Dennis, how far off the ground was I?"

"Hmm . . . ," Dennis said as he took a sip of his soft drink. "I guess if I had moved fast I could have slipped a phone book under your feet."

"You mean a phone *booth,*" Nick said. "I'm telling you, Justin, I had my nose in the ozone layer."

"Okay, okay," Justin interrupted. "You were floating against the gym ceiling, but what happened in the *game*?"

"Just the facts?"

"Just the facts."

"Well, thanks to my passing, Dennis led the scorers with eleven points."

"Twelve," Dennis corrected.

"Okay, twelve, but only because Williamsport was triple-teaming me after I scored seven points in the first half."

"Liar," Sam interrupted, but Nick ignored him.

"I finished with nine points," Nick continued. "Coach G. wanted me to save my energy for the big Bradley game."

"What'd you do, Sam?" Justin asked.

"Me, I, uh . . . well I had more fouls than points."

"The gorilla!" Nick exclaimed.

"I can't help it if I play too tough for those skinny little Williamsport kids."

"What about Pockets? Did he do any better?" No one responded. "That bad, huh?"

"He just doesn't know what to do with himself," Dennis said. "He was fouling left and right and still couldn't hang on to any rebounds. He made a couple shots, though."

They finished up lunch. In practice that afternoon, Nick went out of his way to help Pockets. A solid player at center could make all the difference between a contending team and an also-ran. Nick passed to the gangly center frequently during the scrimmages, and tried to offer friendly encouragement even though Pockets continued to bounce rebounds off his knuckles and throw up bricks for shots.

On Wednesday, the Panthers were scheduled to play Bradley. The win over Williamsport had given them a 2–0 record and they were beginning to gain confidence. If they kept working and improving, they could make a run at the league championship. But Bradley was also undefeated. Alden knew they had gotten by so far on a little luck and some hot shooting. Bradley would be their first real test.

Game time came. For the first ten minutes, Alden

looked as if they were ready to drum Bradley out of the league. They didn't turn the ball over once—not a missed pass or a double dribble—and when the quarter was over they had a handy 11–2 lead.

With the start of the second quarter, though, Alden's momentum slipped away. Bradley snapped off two great passes leading to a quick lay-up. Over the next five minutes of play, all the bounces went Bradley's way. The Alden second string was giving up too many easy chances. Coach G. brought Paul and Nick back in to do the ball handling, but somehow, they couldn't regain the early magic. Alden finally scored again—on a short jump shot by Sam—but Bradley answered with another charge and by halftime they had come all the way back and tied the score: 15–15.

After the break, the starters took the floor again. The subs hadn't been able to hold Bradley back, but the front five had dominated. Now they just had to do it once more.

Kyle led an early Alden charge, playing with terrific energy, but his six points were offset by his second and third personal fouls. Nick intercepted a pass and hit Kyle with a great lead pass, but Kyle took it straight at the defender. They collided as Kyle floated the ball in. The ref blew the whistle.

"No basket!" he said, waving it off. "I got a twenty-two green, for charging."

An offensive foul, and Kyle's fourth personal foul—the limit—so he had fouled out of the game. The play took the steam out of Alden.

Nick tried to take up the slack, but his efforts were only frustrating.

He hit Pockets with a perfect give-and-go, but the center had the ball stripped away.

"Let's get it back, Pockets," Nick said, slapping his back. "Head up. Let's go, D. C'mon, D."

No matter how hard Nick tried, he seemed to mess up. When he tried to shift over and help out on defense, his man got free and went to the hoop. When he passed, it didn't move the team. He ended up forcing shots, and missing them.

Bradley quickly wore down the starters and built a six-point lead. Alden looked less like a team and more like five guys taking turns with the ball. As both sides grew weary in the fourth, the scoring slowed. The final was Bradley 34–Alden 28. While Bradley slapped high fives on their way to the visitors' locker room, Alden slowly and quietly gathered up their sweats. Bradley was 3–0. For Alden, the undefeated season was just a memory.

# 4

"So where did you get a weird nickname like 'Pockets,' anyway?" Nick asked.

He and the center were in the gym early. They had changed into their practice uniforms, but were sitting in the bleachers waiting for Coach to arrive and unlock the ball closet.

"Just some friends at my old school, I guess. I forget," Pockets answered.

"But what does it mean?"

"It's short for Highpockets, you know? Because my legs are so long."

"Oh. Do you like it?"

"I guess so. It's better than Ed."

"Ed is your real name?"

Pockets nodded. Nick mulled it over.

"Maybe you could use a new nickname, maybe that's what's holding you back on the court."

"A new nickname?"

"Yeah, you know why they call Karl Malone 'The Mailman'?"

"Why?"

"Because he *delivers*."

"That's cool," Pockets said.

"I know! We'll call you 'Empire State Building' because you're tall and you don't move around much."

"Very funny. Maybe we should call you 'Barf' because you're all over the floor and you stink."

"That's my dog's name!"

"Your dog?"

"Yeah, Barf, my dog."

"Really?" Pockets asked, laughing. "Your dog's name is Barf? No way."

"It's true," Nick said. "He's my beagle. Of course,

I knew my parents wouldn't let me name him that, so I told them I named him 'Ralph'. He answers to both names."

Coach G. arrived and got out the practice balls. Nick and Pockets started shooting around. They got along really well. Pockets never tired of Nick's wisecracks. They shared a sense of humor, but Nick wished Pockets shared some of his basketball talent as well. It was frustrating to watch Pockets stumble around the court.

As they played, Nick wondered if he could help Pockets work on his game. *The guy has such potential,* Nick thought. *Five foot ten inches at age thirteen—he could be a scoring machine.*

"You get under the basket," Nick said. "I'll keep shooting and you practice grabbing the rebounds and going right back up with them."

Pockets shrugged agreeably and took his place. On the first ball, Pockets got the rebound and tossed it up but hit the underside of the rim. Nick rolled his eyes. They tried a few more. Pockets jammed a finger, but not badly. Then Pockets accidentally threw a pass over Nick's head. Nick retrieved it. Standing at the far side of the court, he started to throw a long pass, but had a better idea.

"Nick Wilkerson needs to hit the tenpin to win," Nick said, going into his announcer voice. He held the basketball like a bowling ball.

"He rolls it," he continued. The ball spun across the court and Pockets played along by standing still, pretending to be the pin. The ball missed.

"Wow!" Pockets said. "Did you see how much that ball curved? Let me try."

He picked up the ball and rolled it back, trying to make it spin. They found that they could make the ball travel in wide arcs across the gym floor. Nick set up some plastic cones to make a slalom course. They then used the cones as targets. Before long, other players arrived and practice began. Nick realized that he and Pockets had goofed away another chance to practice, but "basketbowling" was more fun.

On Friday the Panthers boarded the bus bound for South Colby and their fourth game. Glancing over at South during warm-ups, the Alden players were impressed. South Colby ran tight warm-up drills. They moved in neat lines, made every lay-up and snapped off passes. They even ran a drill where each player went up and bounced the ball off the backboard in midair, with the next player jumping up right behind to bounce it against the backboard again. It looked very cool. In contrast, Alden warm-ups were disorderly and plain. The loss to Bradley had hurt the team's confidence, and South's pregame show wasn't helping any.

At the game's start, South Colby took quick advantage of Alden's shakiness. They scored, intercepted a pass, and scored again. Two plays later, Nick brought the ball upcourt and passed to Paul, who tried to drive inside but had the ball stripped away. South broke free and took it in for a quick lay-up. Nick and Dennis were both running back, but too late to do anything about it.

"I guess that's what they call a fast-break offense, right?" Nick said.

"Save your jokes for the bench," Dennis said angrily. With the team down 6–0, he was in no mood for wisecracks. As team captain, he was doing his best to be a leader, and that meant keeping Nick's shenanigans under control.

Finally, Alden got on the scoreboard as Dennis hit a fifteen-footer. The early jitters began to disappear. The Alden defense now set up properly, arms held high, moving and shutting down lanes. By the end of the first quarter, Alden had closed the gap to three points. Sam, coming off the bench, had made two key shots, and Nick had sunk two as well.

25

The second quarter was a setback. The shooting went stone cold. Alden got desperate, going to the hoop even with blockers right in their faces. When the half ended, South was riding an eight-point lead, 21–13.

Resting on the bench during the half, Nick apologized to Dennis.

"Hey, Dennis. Sorry about that crack about fast breaks."

Dennis shrugged.

"Now he hates me," Nick said playfully, pretending to cry.

"Don't be stupid. I just don't think jokes have any place on the court."

"I'll be serious, Captain Clements. Yessir."

Dennis laughed, but Nick saw his smile fade quickly, so he clammed up. They were in the middle of losing their second straight game.

Nick scored the first basket of the second half with a sweet jumper set up by an even sweeter fake pass. Feeding off his success, Nick took charge, providing his own brand of leadership. He was all energy, bouncing around on defense, yelling and hooting, calling plays and handling the ball on offense. Slowly, Alden gained on South.

With six minutes to play, Alden pulled to within

one basket. South was playing too carefully now. They had been ahead for so long they lost some of their aggressiveness. Their offense passed the ball back and forth, back and forth. Finally, they put up a shot that missed off the front of the rim. Kyle and Pockets both went for it. Nick yelled "Same team!" but too late. Pockets knocked the ball out of Kyle's hand toward one of South's players. Sam jumped in and knocked the ball away, but it headed out of bounds. Nick took a chance. In one motion, he jumped past the endline in the air. He grabbed the ball with one hand and, as he fell, flung it hard back into the court. The nearest South player was too surprised to prevent the ball from hitting him hard in the knee and bouncing out of bounds. Alden's ball!

The Alden bench burst into cheers. "Way to go!" Nick heard someone yell.

Dennis ran out to help Nick up.

"Nice hustle," he said, slapping Nick's back.

The play gave Alden all the momentum they needed. Nick brought the ball up, drove for the basket, then fed the ball back out to Mugsy, who buried the easy jumper to tie the score. For all their snazzy warm-up drills, South was falling apart now. They mishandled the ball, passed it over and back for a violation, and missed the few shots they took.

On the Alden side, Nick was the hot hand, sizzling, in fact. He made three more baskets and two foul shots as they built the lead. The game's final minute ticked off quickly.

Alden had won, 35–29. They were back on the championship trail. Nick led all scorers with sixteen points and everyone congratulated him as they celebrated. Now Dennis could stop worrying. He punched Nick playfully on the shoulder.

"Awesome game."

"Not bad for a wise guy, huh?" Nick asked with a laugh.

# 5

Snow had started falling during the South Colby game. By Saturday morning a foot of heavy powder—perfect for snowballs and forts—blanketed the streets and yards of Cranbrook. When Nick got up to survey the scene from his bedroom window, he was still in a great mood from the win.

Just then Barf jumped up and put his front paws on the windowsill to look out and see what Nick found so interesting. He barked.

"You like the snow, Barf? How 'bout a good romp in it?"

Barf barked again, his tail wagging furiously. He let himself down off the windowsill and ran in excited circles around the room. Nick got dressed quickly. Downstairs, he dug his heavy boots out of the closet and got out Barf's leash.

After a short walk—both Nick and Barf quickly grew tired as they stomped their way through the deep drifts—they returned and Nick's mother made hot cereal for him.

"Sammy McCaskill called while you were out."

"It's not Sammy anymore, just Sam."

"Okay, *Sam*."

"What did he want?"

"I'm getting to that—he's going to the municipal golf course to sled with Dennis and Justin. He said you could meet them there if you liked."

"Great! Can I go?"

"No, I'm sorry. You have to stay and mow the lawn."

"Mow the . . . oh. Very funny, Mom. Can I?"

"Yes, you may."

"Can I take B—Ralph?"

"If you don't stay for too long, I think that would be all right."

"Great! Thanks!"

Nick quickly grabbed a sweater and his ski gloves. Soon he and Barf were making their way through Sapsucker Woods on the path that was a shortcut to the back of the golf course.

By the time he arrived, dragging his plastic sled, Nick could see Sam, Dennis, and Justin, hard at work on building a jump in the middle of the best hill. He snuck around to the top of the hill, pulled his ski goggles on over his glasses, and jumped on his sled to make a grand entrance. He flew down the packed snow on the hill, with Barf yelping and running along. The guys saw him coming.

"Hey! It's not ready yet!" Sam yelled.

"I can't stop!" Nick howled, without trying.

He hit the jump but the sled's front edge caught. Both Nick and sled flipped over, dragging down a bunch of snow from the jump. Even before he landed, Nick knew he had made a mistake. When he finally stopped sliding, Barf was there licking his face.

"I'll fix it, I'll fix it," Nick said quickly. He could tell that his friends were annoyed. "That was really stupid."

"Why don't you go make snow angels or something," Sam said.

31

"Okay," Nick said. He ran off and threw himself on his back in an untouched area of snow, waving his arms and legs. The others laughed.

Nick picked himself up and then helped bring fresh snow from the sides to pile onto the jump. They packed it down carefully with all their weight until it was ready for some test runs. The first runs were disasters. The jump didn't fall apart, but it was way too high. Takeoff was exciting, but it wasn't worth the pain of coming down.

They adjusted the jump so that it was less bone-jarring on the landings.

"I've got an idea," Nick said. "I'll be Evel Knieval and you guys can be cars. You lie down and I'll see if I can jump over all three of you."

"Okay," Sam said.

"No way!" Justin exclaimed.

"I'll get the stunt cycle ready," Nick said, running up the hill.

At the top of the hill, Nick saw his three friends lying beneath the jump. He knew exactly what was going to happen, but he set off anyway.

"Cowabunga!" he yelled as he whizzed toward them.

At the last moment they scurried to their feet and

then just as Nick hit the jump, they leapt aboard in a pileup.

They sledded for a couple of hours and Nick wished he had worn a turtleneck or brought a scarf. It was cold, and running up the hill was making him sweat. Barf seemed to be enjoying himself, though, so Nick stayed a little while longer, then set out for the walk home. It seemed a lot farther going back.

Sunday, Nick was tired, so he went to bed early.

Monday, he had a runny nose, and got really worn out at basketball practice.

Tuesday morning, Mrs. Wilkerson took Nick's temperature.

"Almost a hundred and one," she said. "Right back to bed with you."

"Oh, no, I don't feel that bad."

"I can't believe I'm hearing this. You want to go to school instead of a day of ginger ale, comic books, and TV? You really must be sick."

"I feel fine," Nick protested, but his sore throat was making it hard to sound convincing.

"I know what you're up to, but forget it. There is no way you're going to play in that basketball game tonight."

That evening the Alden Panthers were scheduled to play St. Stephens Junior High.

"Can I just watch the game?"

"If it's on TV."

"Thanks a lot," Nick said glumly.

So Nick had to wait until one of his friends got home from the game to hear how it came out. At ten o'clock Sam phoned.

"Hi, Nick, what's up? My mom said you called."

"What do you think?"

"Uh, you want to know about the game?"

"Brilliant deduction, Sherlock."

"We won."

"Great!"

"They weren't very good."

"What was the score?"

"Um, like 35–14, I think."

"Oh, man," Nick croaked, "I missed our first blow-out. I could have played sick and scored fifteen points, I know it. Who played point guard?"

"Paul did most of the ball-handling. Mugsy played well, too. Zack did okay. A lot of guys did better than usual."

"How'd you do?"

"Not bad, only three fouls. Made a basket, too."

"Who scored all those points? Dennis?"

"Yeah, Dennis had ten or twelve, I guess. Hey, you won't believe who scored a lot. Guess?"

"Mike Dorfman?" Mike was by far the worst player on the team.

"No, not *that* incredible, try again."

"Alex?"

"No. Pockets! He was great, or at least good. He really dominated the rebounds and actually made a batch of shots. He still missed all six of the free throws he took, but hey, at least he made some progress."

"Wow, Pockets scoring, that's good. We could sure use a center."

"No kidding."

"So you won without me, pretty amazing."

"Yeah, there wasn't any goofing around during pregame warm-ups, no cracking jokes on the bench, no clowning around at all. We just got down to business. It was boring without Nick-the-Slick to entertain us."

Nick coughed hoarsely.

"More like Nick-the-Sick," Nick said, beginning to feel tired. "Listen, thanks for calling, Sam. I gotta go. Maybe I'll see you tomorrow and maybe I won't."

"Okay, feel better."

Nick hung up the phone. He was glad Alden had

won, but he wished the team had missed him more. *Why couldn't they have struggled a little bringing the ball up? he thought. Well, St. Stephens is rotten, that's all.*

Because Christmas vacation was coming up, the next game was two whole weeks away. Two weeks sounded like forever to Nick. He wanted to play.

# 6

Coach G. scheduled daily practice during the winter vacation.

Nick was glad to be back in the gym, but with two weeks before the next game, Coach was running real "teaching" practices—loads of drills and individual instruction. They hardly even got a chance to play scrimmage games. Nick wasn't the only one who thought practices were getting boring.

"Hey, Justin," Sam called as they dressed for practice. "What's Coach got in store for us today?"

Justin was carrying a clipboard of his own.

"What do you want to do?" Justin asked.

"How about fifteen minutes of warm-ups and then games?" Sam suggested hopefully.

"That sounds good," Pockets said.

"Not me," Nick chipped in. "How about a half-hour of suicide sprints, lay-up, and passing drills for an hour, and then an hour of practicing zone defense without the ball?"

"That's exactly what you're getting," Justin said.

The players groaned.

"What is the point of all this?" Nick complained. "We're going to forget how to play."

"I think you're right," Paul said. "Coach is drilling us to death."

"He knows what he's doing," Dennis said. "We're 4–1 and tied for first place, right?"

"Dennis is right," Kyle said. "If we're going to take Bradley in our rematch, we've got to practice hard, not piddle around playing scrimmage games."

"You guys are absolutely right," Nick said in a serious tone. "And we need more banzai shot practice, too."

Everyone laughed.

"Yeah," chimed in Pockets. "Maybe we need more basketbowling practice."

A few guys headed out to the court, while the rest were still dressing. Nick pulled on his jock over his boxer shorts. He was the only member of the team, who wore this odd combination of boxers, jock, then gym shorts.

"Why do you wear those long boxers anyway?" Pockets asked. "You want the whole world to see how pretty your underwear is?"

Nick looked around, as though making sure no one was listening, but they all were.

"Look, I'll tell you if you keep it a secret," Nick said.

"Deal."

"Okay," Nick began, speaking in a fake whisper loud enough so everyone could hear him and chuckle some more. "It's part of my secret plan to impress Coach G. I figure that if I *look* like an idiot who barely knows how to dress himself, and then I make a shot or two, he'll say 'Hey, maybe this guy isn't a spaz after all.' If I dressed like a normal guy, then Coach wouldn't even notice when I made some shots. See? Dress stupid, and the way you play looks better."

Everyone smiled at Nick's ridiculous logic as they finished dressing.

"Heck, I'll try anything!" Pockets said, pulling his

elastic shorts halfway up his chest.

Out on the court, Dennis and a couple of other players were already warming up. Coach was scribbling on his clipboard. Then the parade started. Paul came out of the locker room with socks over his sneakers. Mugsy was wearing a T-shirt as shorts. Everyone was wearing something ridiculous.

"I don't know what this is supposed to be," Dennis said, "but I do know that somehow Wilkerson is responsible."

"Good morning, Coach G.," Pockets said, wearing a pair of underwear on his head.

"Good morning, Pockets," said Coach, smiling, but shaking his head at the same time. "All right, the fashion show is over."

The players rearranged their outfits.

Practice was long and hard. Warm-ups, then "suicides"—sprints out to the foul line and back, then to half-court and back, then the far foul line and back, finally the length of the court and back. All the stopping and starting made it much more tiring than just running. The squeaking of sneakers was the only sound in the gym.

As Justin had said, there were no games today. By the end of practice, every player was beat, but

Coach kept running them, barking instructions all the while. They were running a three-man play, one shooter, two rebounders.

"Box him out, Pockets! I don't care if you're seven feet tall, you've got to get in position. Next up!"

"Go straight up, Kyle, you're all over the place."

"Get some arc on that shot, Nick, up with backspin. Up!"

Eventually, Coach had them stop running and made them walk through a zone defense. The idea was to cover an area of the court instead of an opposing player. Tired and bored, Nick made the mistake of pretending to fall asleep when he thought Coach wasn't looking.

"I guess you don't need to listen to this, huh, Wilkerson?"

"Yes—I mean no. Sorry," Nick stuttered.

"I know this isn't fun. It's not supposed to be. Maybe you think you're so much better than everyone else you don't need to bother. You're wrong. Every one of you guys has got to learn fundamental basketball. If you can't take practice seriously, you're just holding the team back."

Nick hung his head and didn't say a word, but he was steamed. *I don't think I'm better than anyone else,* he thought. *Cripes, it was one little thing and he has a conniption.*

Even though he thought Coach was unfair, Nick didn't want to get in any more trouble. He decided to be serious from then on. Come Friday, and Alden's game against North Colby, Coach would see just how valuable a player he was.

# 7

Nick took the inbounds pass from Kevin and turned upcourt. He dribbled slowly, sizing up the North Colby defense, waiting for his man to come out to him.

Sweat dripped from his head. He could feel it on his neck and face. He shook his head back, flipping the wet hair away from his glasses. He was breathing hard, trying to figure out how to get around North's defense.

North Colby was the first team that Alden was

facing for the second time. The schedule called for them to play each of their opponents once at home and once away.

The defending guard met Nick at half-court and Nick turned sideways to him, still dribbling. He could hardly believe that this was the same North team they had beaten 24–20. This game was another story. Late in the third quarter, North led 26–16.

Nick looked over the floor. Pockets had a hand up inside, but there was no way to get a pass to him. Paul was trying to get free, but having no luck. Nick took a long dribble right, then spun left to get past his man, but lost his balance slightly. The North guard took the opening and stripped the ball neatly away and was three steps downcourt before Nick got his balance back. Nick started after him but quickly saw it was hopeless. A whole long game of watching North score had worn him down. He stopped chasing in frustration, stood up straight and then gave a little bye-bye wave.

Right away, Nick knew he'd made a mistake. The North man missed the lay-up, and the next man to get there was the other North guard, who put it in. *If I had kept running,* Nick thought, *I could have gotten that rebound.*

"Time out!" bellowed Coach G., who had caught

Nick's little wave and was not amused. He walked angrily out onto the court.

"Funny man, Wilkerson."

"I'm sorry."

"Sit. Mugsy in at guard. Kratchman in for O'Brien."

Nick sat on the far end of the bench. He knew he had messed up. He still didn't see why Coach had to come down on him so hard. *I made one mistake. Maybe I'm a wise guy,* he thought. *That's just my personality. Sometimes it's good, sometimes it's bad.*

Nick watched from the bench in frustration as Alden tried to catch up, but it was looking more and more hopeless as time ticked away. Alden scored two baskets, but North still led, 30–22. North's starters were on the bench. Even against the second string, Alden couldn't score fast enough.

Then, with five minutes left, Nick heard Coach bark his name.

"You ready to play?"

Nick was surprised.

"Uh, yes, sir, sure."

"Keep your head in the game."

"Yes, sir."

Coach put him in with the next round of substitutions. Nick wanted to do well. He wanted to prove himself to Coach. On the first possession he tried to go to the hoop, but North was all over him. With two men on him, he knew someone was free. Slyly, Nick held his dribble, pretending to be trapped. The two defenders moved in, surrounding him, but Nick pivoted free and jumped in the air with the ball cocked. He knew he had only a split second to find the open man, and he did, seeing Kyle's hand up inside. Nick fired the pass in. Kyle caught it and hit the lay-up.

For the next two minutes, Nick rocked the court, playing the toughest offensive basketball he could. Alden caught up, tying the score with two minutes to play. Nick kept it going. He sank two jumpers, made a steal, and collected an offensive rebound. When the final buzzer sounded, the Panthers had won, 45–33.

Nick was first in line to shake hands with the North Colby players. His teammates were loudly hooting and slapping hands, but before he could celebrate, Nick had an apology to deliver. He walked over to Coach Gimigliano.

"Coach? I'm sorry about the wave."

"All right, Nick. It's just that there's a time and place for jokes. Right?"

"Right."

46

"You played well. This team needs your energy, Nick."

"Thanks."

Nick walked off, relieved. Coach wasn't so angry after all. After getting yelled at in practice twice that week, Nick was afraid he was really going to get stuck with a bad reputation. He was glad that Coach could see that he was a good ballplayer, besides being a wise guy.

# 8

While Alden prepared for their next game against arch-rival Lincoln, they were cocky. They were talking championship, but Justin had his doubts.

"What are you worrying about, Justin?" Sam said, bouncing the playground ball with one hand. Along with Nick and Dennis, they were playing four-square behind the school during their lunch-hour break. Grids were painted on the blacktop especially for the game. Four-square was simple: each player had to return any ball bounced in his square to one of the others.

"We've got a great team," Sam continued. "Lincoln doesn't stand a chance."

"Lincoln is a lot better than North and we almost lost to them," Justin responded.

" 'Almost' means nothing," Nick said sincerely. "We won."

"Yeah, but . . ."

"C'mon, Justin, lighten up. We've got talent to burn. If we played North again, we'd massacre them."

"That's just the problem—you guys have *too much* confidence."

"C'mon, let's play," Nick said. Sam served.

"You're tough on us, Justin," Dennis said as he reached out to return Sam's serve.

"Yeah, Mr. Team Manager, besides overconfidence, what's wrong with our team?" Nick asked, watching Sam hit back to Dennis again. "We've got the horses, we can run, shoot, score. We're simply better than the other guys in this league."

Dennis lightly deflected the ball and Justin lunged to get the dink shot and sent it back to Nick.

"Nothing's wrong, exactly." Justin paused to return the ball again. "But I've watched you guys all season and you practice like you're showing off instead of getting ready for games."

"Oh no," Nick said. "Not another 'be more serious' speech. You and Captain Dennis here."

"We wouldn't have to lecture you all the time if you weren't so hyper," Dennis protested.

Sam jumped back to get the ball, but hit it out, losing the point.

"Forget I said anything," Justin said. "If Coach thinks you should practice more seriously, he'll say something. I'm sure you'll whip Lincoln. Okay?"

"Too late," Nick said, serving the ball to Justin. "You *doubted* us!"

"It's get-Justin time," Sam smirked.

Justin hit across to Dennis, but even though Dennis agreed with him about practicing more seriously, he hit it right back. No matter whom he tried, Justin got the ball back, but he was gamely making shot after shot. Just then the bell ending lunch period sounded. The ball came to Justin and he caught it.

"We'll continue this game tomorrow," he said, triumphantly. He had withstood the bombardment without losing the point. The other three slapped him on the back.

Nick and Pockets were the first ones at practice that afternoon. While Pockets sat on the floor stretching, Nick played announcer as he dribbled up court.

"It's Nick Wilkerson bringing the ball up. The young point guard holds the hopes of the Alden Panthers in his hands. Just twenty seconds left on the clock. He's under pressure! But he spins away— a positively dazzling display of basketball wizardry! Ten seconds left. He zigs, he zags, he's going to the hoop. Five seconds. He stops, he goes up. Three, two, he shoots—"

"And misses!" Pockets yelled.

"But there's still time on the clock as he collects his own rebound."

"And the buzzer sounds. It's over."

"No, he shoots again."

"Too late. Wilkerson costs Alden the game."

"It's good! The Panthers win! The Panthers win! The Panthers win!"

Nick was in high spirits. So was the whole team. They were 5–1, and getting better with every practice. Anyone could see the difference. Not everything Coach G. tried to teach them was working, but they were shooting more consistently, handling the ball with more control, and learning how to maintain good defensive position. Everyone was psyched for the Lincoln game.

Dennis was particularly intense in practice, taking his role as team captain seriously. He couldn't get *too* serious though, or Nick would go into his obedient-soldier bit, snapping to attention and saluting: "YES, SIR! NO, SIR, SIR!"

Practice got under way. After the usual warm-up drills, they were practicing a 2–1–2 zone defense. As Kevin brought the ball up, Nick was on defense, covering the front right area of the key.

Nick went out to Kevin, pressuring him. Kevin passed over to Jeremy. The ball went around. The offense wasn't used to playing against a zone. They didn't know how to attack it. Finally, Paul took a pass and went up with the shot.

But Nick was there. Leaping high in the air from the side, Nick swiped at the ball just as it left Paul's hands, sending it flying out of bounds.

"In yo' face!" Nick taunted, the moment he hit the floor.

"All right," Coach G. said, stepping in. "That was a nice piece of blocking, but you can't really do that. Get back in the positions you were in before the shot."

52

Coach placed them again and gave the ball to Kyle.

"Now watch Kyle move in, and the center and forward are both on him, so he passes back. So far so good. But now, even though Zack here is in bad position, Nick can't afford to come help out, because if he does—go ahead, come out to block like you did—okay, freeze. Look at the situation. Both guards and the center are forward and crowding the right side. All I have to do is get it over to the left side."

He demonstrated by making a pass to Kevin.

"And boom. A three-on-one situation until we can get back in shape. Let's walk through it again."

Coach flipped the ball to Kyle. Kyle moved in, then passed back to Paul. Nick came over as he had, but faked going up for the block. He stayed in position, so that when Paul tried to get the ball left, he was there to intercept the pass.

"Okay, Nick, very funny. That goes to show that if you know exactly what the offense is going to do, then it's easy to play defense. One more time."

Kyle took the ball again, moved in, then instead of passing the ball back to Paul, he faked the pass and easily went by Alex to shoot the ball up and in.

"I've got a team full of comedians," Coach G. said, shaking his head but smiling. "All right, let's *not* run through this play again, but don't forget the main point here: the zone doesn't allow you to jump around as much as you might think."

They switched and ran some passing drills, then Coach put them back into the zone.

"Okay, this is the 2–1–2 again, but Kyle, put the ball down. Yeah, just set it aside. We're going to practice *position*, not ball watching."

Coach set them up and had the offense pretend to pass the ball around while the defense shifted to cover.

"That's it, arms up, a defense! Don't cross your legs, Pockets, side-to-side. All right, just keep moving it around. I'll be right back."

Coach went to the sideline, leaving them alone.

They kept running the drill for a while, but playing without a ball seemed really weird to Nick.

"I feel like I'm at a square dance," Nick cracked as he followed his man out and then back again. The others laughed.

Nick grabbed his man by the arm and spun around.

"Spin your partner, round and round," Nick said. Then he pretended to be playing a fiddle. "Do-si-do! Curlicue!"

The others joined in. The drill fell apart completely. They were all laughing until they saw the look on Coach's face.

He was fuming.

They realized they were in trouble and tried to regroup and start up the drill, but it didn't work. The gym grew quiet, quieter than Nick had ever heard it.

"Basketball is a very funny game," Coach G. said in a calm but stern voice. "A lot of laughs, I guess. I can't leave you alone for one minute!"

His voice rose angrily. "What in tarnation are you guys doing here? It sure isn't practicing ball!"

He paced silently.

"You should have told us to knock it off," Dennis mumbled apologetically.

"What?"

"You should have told us to knock it off."

"Do you know how many times I've told you guys to knock it off, to quiet down, to shut up? That's all I do around here and I'm tired of it. I'm here to teach basketball, not run a kindergarten."

He paced some more. No one dared say anything.

"Here's what we'll do. Forget the zone defense. The eighth-grade team uses it, but I guess you guys aren't old enough yet. Forget it. It's out of the playbook."

For the rest of practice, the team was silent. Coach G. had really knocked the wind out of them.

"I guess you warned us, Justin," Dennis said afterward in the locker room.

"No kidding," Nick agreed. "I had no idea Coach was getting so ticked off. I guess we have to cancel those plans to spend tomorrow's practice learning to spin the ball on one finger."

"Very funny," Dennis said. "You never learn, do you, Nick?"

"Oh, this is all my fault, is it?"

"I didn't say that. Everyone has been goofing around too much, basketbowling, betting baseball cards on shots, all that stuff."

"Well, the captain has spoken," Nick said sarcastically. Dennis was embarrassed.

"C'mon, Nick," Justin said, trying to ease the growing tension.

"I'm not trying to lecture," Dennis said. "I just want to win games."

Dennis was dressed, so he and Justin left, leaving Sam and Nick alone.

"Was it something I said?" joked Nick.

Sam chuckled. "They'll get over it."

"I just don't see what the fuss is all about."

"I know that. But sometimes you've got to get serious."

"I've played well all season."

"Sure, you scored a lot of points, but maybe if you weren't clowning around half the time you'd be even better."

"Only one thing wrong with that," Nick said with a smile.

"What's that?"

"If I was any better, I'd be downright dangerous."

Sam laughed. "You never stop, do you, Nick?"

"Nope," Nick smiled.

# 9

"Hold it, nobody move."

Nick held out his hands. Pockets, Sam, and Justin all looked at him. They were sitting around a table eating lunch in the school cafeteria.

"I'm not sure," Nick said, staring at his hot lunch tray. "But I think my meat loaf is alive. There! It moved, did you see it!"

The others laughed as Nick stabbed it with his fork and shook it.

"Hey don't mess it up," Sam said. "I'll eat that."

"No way," Nick said. "I killed it—I get to eat it."

Dennis approached the table, carrying some books, a bag lunch, and a pint of milk. Pockets pulled out a chair for him, but just as Dennis sat down, he kicked it away. Dennis realized too late and lost his balance, falling hard to the floor. His books scattered.

"Oww! You stupid dork!" Dennis yelled angrily.

"Are you okay? I'm sorry," Pockets stuttered. "I didn't think you'd actually fall."

"I ought to whale on you," Dennis said, making a fist.

"One free shot," said Pockets, grimacing in expectation. Dennis punched his shoulder hard.

"Oww," Pockets said, helping Dennis pick up his books and papers.

"Pockets," Dennis said. "If they stuffed your brain up an ant's nose, it would roll around like a BB in a boxcar."

"It was just a joke."

"And very funny, too," Dennis said. "You've been hanging around Nick too much."

"Oh, no," Nick said with a laugh. "Don't blame me. I get in enough trouble on my own."

Dennis sat down and opened his milk.

"Speaking of trouble," he said, "do you guys think Coach G. is really going to dump the zone defense?"

"He sure wasn't happy about it," Sam said.

"He'll probably keep us off it a week and then bring it back," Pockets said.

"Unless we have another square dance," Nick said, but no one laughed.

"Hey, Nick, I think I could make it if you guys are going to play ball Saturday," Dennis said. Last Saturday, Nick had tried to get his pals to come play basketball at the YMCA gym.

"Yeah, maybe we'll do that. Last week Pockets and I were the only ones that made it."

"Was the gym empty?" Sam asked.

"Yeah, but we ended up playing pool," Pockets said.

"Hey, don't tell them that," Nick said. "We practiced really hard, yep, sure did."

"Oh man, Pockets and his personal coach," Sam said.

"Yeah," Dennis agreed with a laugh, "Pockets learning all the basics: how to pull out someone's chair, the use of the whoopie cushion, how to imitate the Harlem Globetrotters. Great."

"Well, excu-u-u-se me," Pockets said. "We do play basketball every day. I'm getting better."

"I'm just kidding, Pockets," Dennis said. The warning bell rang and they wolfed down the remains of their lunches. Dennis and Nick had their next class together, so they walked there together.

"You were pretty rough on Pockets," Nick said. "He is getting better."

"But he's still pretty rotten," Dennis responded.

"That's true."

"Why don't you really work with him? The guy is huge. He could be great. You're always talking about practicing with him."

"I've tried, but it's hard."

"I know and then you spend all day shooting pool."

"Since when is Pockets my personal responsibility?"

"I thought you wanted to help him, that's all."

"I do."

"All you've taught him is how to be a wise guy."

"Well, that's an important start."

Dennis had to laugh.

They arrived at their English class. Mr. Abernathy had given out assigned seats, so they weren't near each other. Nick thought about Pockets. He wondered if he could made a difference. There was so little extra time, what with practice every day, and homework and stuff.

Nick hadn't even started the reading for today's class: George Orwell's *Animal Farm*. As Mr. Abernathy checked the attendance, Nick cracked open his paperback behind his desk. He scanned the third chapter, looking for something to say in case he got called on. Unfortunately, he didn't have enough time. Mr. Abernathy asked what the class thought of the book so far. Then he ignored the raised hands and zeroed in on Nick.

"Nick?"

Nick tried to look composed.

"I think," he said, "I think we're a little old to be reading a book about talking pigs."

A few giggles. Nick hoped that would do.

"Is it about talking pigs?"

*I haven't the slightest idea,* thought Nick, but he had to say something. "Well, it has pigs and the pigs talk, so yes, I would say so."

More chuckles.

"You haven't read it, have you, Nick?"

"No, sir."

"I suggest you do so by tomorrow. Now, this is a book with pigs as characters, but does anyone have a more thoughtful idea what it is about?"

Nick sank in his seat. *At least it was over quickly,* he thought. He looked at the clock and figured out the exact number of minutes until basketball practice. One hundred seven and counting.

# 10

Coach G. held to his promise. No zone defense at practice. Furthermore, he ran them and drilled them like never before. Practices were dead serious. Even Nick found the atmosphere too heavy for joking. Coach's harsh outburst early in the week had subdued the team. Still, when the Panthers dressed to play Lincoln, they were optimistic. They felt ready.

Coach had made a change for today's game. Pockets O'Brien had been demoted from the starting five. No one was too surprised. The big guy just hadn't done the job. Nick guessed the move was meant as a wake-up call to Pockets. Coach obviously didn't think he was working hard enough to merit the starting slot.

Pockets was definitely unhappy, but he didn't bellyache. When Alden took the floor for the opening jump ball he was rooting and talking it up like everyone else on the bench.

Lincoln tipped the ball and controlled it.

Nick backpedaled, shuffling his feet to position himself in front of the Lincoln's guard, a red-haired kid who wore number eight. The pass went low to the other side. He glanced at his opponent's face, watching his eyes to determine where he was heading. The kid had an odd expression, a sort of constant smirk.

The ball was passed back out and in again and their forward took a midrange shot. Nick turned and boxed out. The ball bounced off the front of the rim and Nick jumped after it. He got there first, grabbed the rebound, and came down with his elbows out, protecting the ball. Lincoln retreated to their end of the court as Nick dribbled the ball down.

As he approached the top of the foul circle, number eight began to cover him tightly. Nick looked to pass and found Kyle with a bounce. Alex tried to set a pick, but the defenders called out "Switch" and exchanged men. Kyle looked to shoot, but his man was in his face. Finally, he swung the ball back out to Nick.

Nick was ready. The moment the ball hit his hands he snapped it inside to Paul, who had snuck around his man. Paul took it and went up for a short jumper. He swished it and Alden took the lead. As they ran back on defense, Nick and Paul slapped hands.

After another Lincoln miss, Nick tried an outside shot himself and missed. Lincoln came back and Alex committed a foul on the shooter. Fortunately, the guy missed both shots. The next time down the floor Alden scored on Dennis's long jumper.

Everything went Alden's way in the first quarter. They played tough defense and made a good percentage of their shots. Lincoln had done a good job of shutting down Alden's passing game, but Dennis had a hot hand on the outside shots. Alden built a 10–5 lead.

During the second quarter, even as substitutes came in on both sides, Alden held steady. Coach G. kept pushing them to go inside, to work the passes around, but the only open shots they could get were from outside. Pockets came in, and though he took no shots, he pulled down a few tough rebounds. He was out to prove that he was giving a hundred percent effort. At the end of the half, Alden still led, 21–16.

Over the halftime, the hot hands cooled.

As quick and obvious as a light switch, Alden's outside shooting turned off. Dennis missed three. Nick and Kyle two apiece. Just like that, Lincoln was even with them at twenty-one apiece. Coach G. called time out.

"How many times are you going to put the ball up from twenty-five feet?" Coach said in a firm tone. "That's no shot. There aren't any three-point shots in this league, and I wouldn't want you guys to shoot 'em if you could."

He paused a moment, looking around at the players.

"I know it worked in the first half, but it's no mystery why you're missing now. What have I told you a hundred times? Shooting is seventy-five percent legs. You're tired. Your legs aren't getting you up, or letting you set. If you're wobbling around on spaghetti it doesn't matter how sweet a touch you've got in your wrist."

One of the two referees approached their huddle. "Time's up, Coach."

"Thanks. All right, let's move the ball around and

look for that open man in the low post. The *low* post,"
Coach repeated. "Kevin and Mugsy go in for Paul
and Nick."

Over the next few minutes, Alden carefully
worked the ball around and tried to go inside. The
lead went back and forth. Lincoln by a point, then
Alden by a point. When Nick went back in, it was
Lincoln 28, Alden 27.

On the offense, Nick held the ball, searching for
an opening. He found nothing and finally had to go
back out to Zack, who almost lost the ball, but then
got off a pass to Alex, Nick darted inside, across the
paint and back out behind Alex, who dumped the
ball to him. Nick was free for the shot and went up.
The forward who had been on Alex made a desperate
attempt to block and whacked Nick's wrist. The shot
was off, but the referee's whistle blew. Fouled while
shooting. Two shots.

Nick took his place at the foul line, drying his
hands on his shorts. The other players stepped into
their slots around the key. Directly to Nick's right
was his man, number eight.

One referee stood in foul territory under the net.
He flipped the ball out to Nick, who took it, bounced
it once, twice, and put it up. It swished through. The
referee picked up the ball and tossed it back out to

him. As Nick caught it, number eight spoke to him quietly.

"Supposed to check the ball with the other ref," he said quickly, giving a small nod in the direction of the referee who was standing behind and to the side. Flustered, Nick turned and flipped the ball to the ref.

*That's not right,* he thought at the moment he released the ball.

The referee was surprised, giving Nick a puzzled look as he caught the ball. A confused murmur, and some laughs could be heard from the bench and the small crowd. Nick was even more flustered.

"Something wrong?" the ref asked.

"Uh, he . . ." Nick started, but then realized that trying to explain would only complicate things. "No, no problem, sorry."

The referee smiled as he tossed the ball back. Nick glanced at his teammates on the bench. They were all laughing. He then stole a look at the red-haired kid, but he was looking away like nothing had happened. Nick tried to regain his concentration, but he missed the second shot.

As Lincoln brought the ball up, Nick's reaction changed from being flustered to wanting revenge. *Who is this wise guy, anyway?* he thought. Nick tried to stay cool. Now was no time to mess up, but he couldn't resist taking one shot at revenge. As number eight changed directions, going to the left-hand dribble, Nick flicked a hand out quickly, tapping the ball. The Lincoln guard tried to regain control, but Nick stripped the ball away. He sped downcourt and hit the lay-up to give Alden a two-point lead.

Running back down the court, Nick crossed paths with number eight. He couldn't resist a quick smile and wink to rub in his victory. Number eight didn't appreciate Nick's humor. He looked steamed. *The one thing a wise guy can't stand is another wise guy,* Nick thought.

At the next break, a substitute came in for number eight. Lincoln scored to tie it up. Each team then missed two chances more and the third quarter came to an end tied, 30–30.

In the short break between quarters, the guys on the bench were still having a laugh about Nick's "pass." For once, Nick was not enjoying the chuckles.

"So, Nick, did you think the ref was feeling left out?" Justin asked with a laugh.

Nick ignored him.

"Maybe it was just part of his 'Bad Globetrotter' act?" Max said.

Nick gave him a sarcastic smile.

"Maybe . . ." Sam began.

"Shut up, okay?" Nick cut him off. "It wasn't that funny."

The seriousness in his voice made the others stop short. They hadn't often heard Nick sound so annoyed.

In the fourth quarter, Alden began to fade. The inside game closed up, and the outside shots weren't falling. Lincoln scored, and scored again. Coach G. tried to mix starters with players fresh off the bench, but it didn't help. In bursts, Alden outplayed them, but Lincoln was tough and steady. Any time Alden floated a pass, Lincoln was there to pick it off. Any time they stumbled on defense, Lincoln took advantage. With three minutes to go, Lincoln led 41–34.

Lincoln had the ball. The shot went up. Nick turned to position himself for the long rebound, but the ball came off the rim the other way. The moment he saw that the rebound would be on the other side, he was suddenly slammed—a full body check and an elbow in the gut all at once. As he went down he saw his attacker: Lincoln's number eight. In that split second, Nick knew it was no accident.

He was hit so hard he flew across the floor, lost his balance, lost his glasses, rolled over on his back, and ended up on his hands and knees gasping for breath. When he looked up, he couldn't believe two things. First, there was no call, both referees had totally missed the foul. Kyle had made the rebound and Alden had the ball. Second, everyone was waiting for him to get up. Paul was dribbling and smiling at him. Why didn't they call time or something? Third, he glanced at the bench and saw his teammates *laughing*. What did they think? After calling time-out himself, picking up his glasses and going to the bench, he found out.

"What a ham!"

"You deserve an Oscar for that performance!"

"You're okay, right?" Coach G. asked.

"Oh, sure," Nick said, even though he was not at all sure. *They thought he had faked it!* Coach went to the scorer's table to argue that they shouldn't be charged for the time-out. The players were left alone.

"Oh, man, Nick," Sam said. "I've never seen anyone take a spill like that to get the ref to call a foul. What a hoot!"

"I wasn't faking it," Nick fumed. "Didn't anyone see that red-haired guy hit me?"

His teammates looked uncertain for a moment, but grins soon spread across their faces.

"You liar."

"What a kidder."

"No, I'm totally serious," Nick said firmly, but the more he protested, the more they laughed. Nick was bewildered. Finally he just smiled along with them, trying to ignore the throbbing pain in his knee and shoulder. After Coach returned with a few words of advice, he sent them back out. Nick didn't dare ask to sit out.

Playing out the last minutes, Lincoln's defense tightened. Alden found it impossible to score. It was an embarrassment. The final score was Lincoln 45, Alden 36.

As Nick's head cleared and the initial pain eased during the last minutes of the game, he wondered at his team's reaction. *What do you have to do around here to make people realize you're not kidding?* Nick thought. *Get your head knocked off?*

# 11

Nick was early to practice Monday afternoon. He got a ball and started taking foul shots. He kept track of his shooting in his head. Four out of ten. Six out of ten. Six again. Then eight out of ten. Pockets arrived.

"Hey, Nick, what's going on?"

Nick gave him a nod and took another shot.

"How about some basketbowl?" Pockets suggested.

"No thanks."

"C'mon. I'm gonna kill you today. I'll bet you a buck I win."

"I'm practicing, okay? Why don't you do the same?"

Pockets watched as Nick missed. Then he jumped up to grab the rebound and put up a hook shot. He missed and Nick took the ball and walked back to the free-throw line.

"What's the point of practicing hook shots," Nick asked. "You'd never use one in a game." He shot again, making the basket. Pockets grabbed the ball and dribbled out to half-court.

"What'll you give me if I make it from here? C'mon, I'm feeling hot."

"Nothing," Nick said. He walked over to the ball rack and took out another ball.

"Well, excu-u-u-se me," Pockets said. "Aren't we grouchy today?"

"You want to get back in the starting five . . ." Nick began, but he didn't finish the sentence. He didn't have to. Pockets got the message. He dribbled slowly to the far basket, leaving Nick alone.

Nick bounced the ball twice, concentrating. He didn't want to fool around. As a matter of fact, he didn't feel much like talking to anyone. He shot. Swish.

As the other players arrived they were bluntly met

with the "new" Nick. After shooting a hundred foul shots, he ran the length of the court, from basket to basket, shooting lay-ups. His teammates stood around as they usually did before practice and looked at each other in disbelief.

When Nick stopped running and sat down in the bleachers, Dennis sat down with him.

"What's with the before-practice drills?" Dennis asked. "It's not like you."

Nick shrugged.

"You seem like you're in a rotten mood."

"I'm not."

"Well, what is it, then?"

"Just tense, I guess."

"It'd be good to be more serious, but you don't have to become a maniac."

Dennis was going to continue when Coach G. arrived and called for the players' attention.

As Coach reviewed the Lincoln game, pointing out various areas he wanted to improve, Nick's mind wandered. He thought again about the Lincoln cheap shot that knocked him down. How could his teammates have thought he was faking?

But it didn't really seem important anymore. What *was* important was that Nick was tired of playing the clown, and that weekend he decided to change. Everyone—Coach, Dennis, Justin—wanted him to be more serious. *All right,* he had made up his mind. *I'll play it their way. No more banzai shots. No more behind-the-back passes. If that's what it takes to win, I'll do it. Anyway, none of that old stuff seems so funny anymore.*

Coach G. got practice going. By now, the players knew the routine of warm-ups and could do it themselves.

Sam rebounded a lay-up, and saw Nick was next in the shooting line. Instead of passing the ball, he ran a step toward Nick and stuck the ball in his chest.

"Handoff!" Sam said.

Nick just took the ball, took one dribble, and shot. He knew Sam expected him to pretend to be a running back, to play along with the gag. *Tough.*

Sam walked over to Nick as they shifted to the next drill.

"What's the matter, Nick, did Barf die or something?"

"No."

"Yeesh, I was just kidding."

"Uh-huh."

Nick couldn't help it if his new attitude was putting people off. He had to concentrate. He knew that

76

the minute he let down his guard, he would be right back where he started.

The rest of practice was intense. Without Nick's wisecracks, there wasn't much talk at all.

The next day at lunch, Nick looked for his friends in the cafeteria.

"What's the deal, Nick?" Dennis asked the minute Nick sat down.

"What?"

"We've just been sitting here trying to figure out what you're doing. You've turned into 'Joe Serious' overnight."

"Just in practice, that's all. Look, here's my funniest face."

Nick made a halfhearted face. No one laughed. Nick shrugged.

"C'mon, Nick, I know we bugged you to be more serious," Justin said, "but you've gone too far."

"All right, all right," Nick began. "I can't help it. It's all or nothing. We shouldn't have lost to Lincoln—that ticked me off. So I've got to try a new attitude. We've all got to bear down in practice. That's all. I'll try not to be a jerk about it, okay?"

They nodded, but Nick could see they weren't quite sure. He wasn't sure himself, but he knew this was something he had to do. He loved a good laugh, but

Nick was also a competitor. The loss to Lincoln had dropped their record to 5–2. Lincoln and Bradley had better records and South was also 5–2. If Alden was going to stay in the run for the title, they couldn't afford to lose again.

Over the next few days, the team got used to Nick's new attitude. They were no longer surprised when Nick turned down a little one-on-one so he could take jumper after jumper from the corners of the key, or when he wandered away from the conversation to practice dribbling left-handed all by himself. The other guys began to follow his lead. Without the goofing off, practices were relentless workouts of drill after drill.

It wasn't much fun, but Nick could see that it was beginning to pay off. The little things that Coach had lectured about and worked on all season—protecting the ball on rebounds, shuffle steps instead of crossing their legs on defense, good low dribbles under pressure—were finally coming together.

Game day arrived and South Colby showed up at the Alden gym, looking for revenge. Since losing to Alden in their first meeting, South had been on a roll, running their record up to 5–2. Loss or no, they believed they now had the better team.

Alden scored first, on a Paul Sacks drive, but it

was the only lead Alden held for the rest of the first half. South was tough. Very tough. Just when it seemed that Alden had been able to shut down one of their scorers, another player would get the hot hand. Throughout the half Alden played catch-up ball. Only two brief spurts of hot shooting by Nick and Paul kept it from turning into a complete blow-out. At the half, they trailed 24–13.

On the halftime bench, the Panthers quietly tried to regroup.

"These guys aren't *that* good," Dennis said.

"We're playing *their* style," Paul added. "We've got to play aggressive offense like we usually do."

Nick listened but didn't say anything. Then Coach called for their attention.

"All right, listen up," he began. "We're getting run off the floor for no good reason. You look nervous out there. You can't be afraid to make a mistake. Loosen up! Help out on defense. Jump around. Have some fun! Get creative on offense—that's our game."

Nick felt strange, as if he wasn't a part of the team. He couldn't understand why Coach suddenly wanted them to "have fun" after being on his case all season to be more serious. They just had to buckle down and tough it out. This is what basketball is about— guts in crunch time. Nick clenched his fists. He was determined to bring the team back, even if he had to do it all by himself.

South came out for the second half cocky. They had the big lead, and Alden was showing no life. Even after they traded baskets twice, the South players were still grinning and hooting. Then Pockets blocked a shot and a nifty pass from Kyle to Paul earned a quick two. South 32, Alden 27. South came back down and drew a foul, but missed both tries from the penalty line.

Alden was back on track. The defense came together, shutting down South's inside game, forcing them to shoot from outside. On offense, Alden still wasn't playing an exciting game, but they were getting the job done. Dennis was particularly effective, coming down with rebounds on both ends of the court. Nick still felt out of rhythm, missing his shots, but he was passing well.

The score grew closer, but so did the end of the game. Time ticked away. With just one minute left, South led by one point, 41–40. Alden had the ball, but after passing it around for too long, Kyle missed. Dennis was there for the rebound, but so was South's center. The ref called a jump ball. Dennis didn't have a chance. South went on the offense, but they, too, failed to convert. With twenty-eight seconds left,

Alden would have one last chance.

Nick brought the ball up and passed to Paul. Paul spun and tried to drive but the ball was knocked away. Dennis and a South man dove for the ball, but neither could come up with it. Everyone was out of position. The ball bounded away until the South guard grabbed and controlled it. For a moment, the Alden bench groaned, but the guy didn't see Nick right behind him and in a slick move, Nick stripped the ball away.

With the defense spread all over, Nick looked to drive to the hoop. The way was clear, but as he made his jump to lay it up, he was pushed from behind. The ref blew his whistle. Foul. Pockets put out an arm to pull Nick up. As Nick got up he looked at the clock. There was one second left. South 41, Alden 40.

As Nick took his place at the foul line he couldn't help but think of the hundreds of times that he had pretended to be in just this situation while playing in his driveway. Now it was for real. He had two chances: Make both, they win. Make one, they tie. Miss both, they lose.

The ref passed him the ball. When Nick held it in his hands it felt heavy. A flash of fear passed through him. He tried to compose himself, spinning the ball in both hands. He bent his knees, flexing, looking at the hoop. He bounced the ball once, and shot.

It hit the front of the rim. Then the backboard. Then the side of the rim, and fell out. Nick clenched his teeth. His teammates gave a few quiet claps of encouragement.

"Get this one, Nick," Dennis murmured.

"Do it," Kyle said.

Again he spun the ball, waiting for his body to settle. His mind raced. He bounced it once, and yet again. *Concentrate,* he thought, *concentrate.* Then he shot. Nick knew it was bad when it left his hands. The shot clanked off the front rim. South Colby nabbed the rebound and Alden lunged after it, but the final second ticked away and the game was over.

Nick lay in bed that night, replaying the final seconds again and again. He had the ball in his hands, the whole game in his hands and he couldn't make a shot. It wasn't the way it was supposed to be. He should have made them both, been carried around the gym on his teammates' shoulders, cut down the nets as the crowd roared his name. It was supposed to happen in slow motion with big, triumphant music. But it didn't.

Maybe if he had been really serious earlier in the season, things would have been different. Coach and

Dennis had been right. Instead of mastering basketbowling Nick should have been taking extra shots from the line. He should have helped Pockets. None of it made much difference now. But it did! Nick was determined to dedicate himself to basketball. More practice. More concentration.

But even as Nick told himself to be more serious, a small question began to bother him. Would the old Nick—the relaxed, cool, funny, cocky Nick—have made those foul shots?

# 12

The Williamsport gym was the largest Alden had seen. The junior high didn't have their own gym, so they played games at Williamsport High School. Everything was big. The scoreboard was big. The ceiling was immense. The stands, though still mostly empty at game time, were stacked high.

"C'mon, boys, don't let this fancy gym scare you," Coach said, in his pregame pep talk. "That rim is still ten feet off the floor and eighteen inches across. The game is still basketball. Got it?"

The game started slowly, with both defenses dominating. The players were on their toes, arms in the air, cutting off every possible inside passing lane. Alden drew first blood, a twenty-footer by Kyle.

Three baskets later Williamsport was still scoreless. Down 8–0, their spirits were broken. They scored on a fast break, but they just couldn't seem to turn things around. Coming off the bench for Alden, Pockets was playing great. He was all over the court, tough on D, unstoppable under the hoop. Once it was clear that he had the hot hand, his teammates were happy to feed him pass after pass. Even the shots he shouldn't have taken were going in.

Nick, on the other hand, was having his most frustrating game yet. Twice he had the ball stolen from him. The few shots he had taken were bricks—bad misses. He just didn't have any energy. Instead of making plays work on offense, he found himself dishing off the ball because he couldn't see anything to do with it. When Coach substituted Kevin for him near the end of the first quarter Nick was glad. He didn't feel like playing basketball, and anyway, Williamsport was just rolling over. He couldn't get up for them.

By the time the half drew to a close, Nick had been in again for five minutes, but hadn't scored. Sam had thirteen points and the Panthers led, 25–8. To start the second half, Coach G. brought everybody in off the bench.

With the second-stringers on the court, the quality of the game went down a notch, but they scored enough to keep Williamsport out of range.

Sam and Nick were next to each other, watching from the bench.

"You know," Sam said under his breath, "Zack and Mike and all those guys are really doing okay. They've really gotten better."

"Huh? I guess," Nick said.

"Not even watching, huh?"

"No, I was watching," Nick snapped angrily.

"Just kidding," Sam said, looking at Nick in surprise. "Can't you take a joke anymore?"

Alden held their comfortable margin for the rest of the game. Nick got back in for six minutes and continued to struggle. His head just wasn't in the game. Unlike the guys off the bench, who were relishing the opportunity to play for more than two minutes at a time, most of the regulars were playing without great enthusiasm. Williamsport had no bark and no bite. Nick and the other starters weren't having fun. They just wanted to collect the win and go home.

The final score was 36–19. Alden had won again, bringing their record up to a very solid 6–3 with three games remaining. Afterward they congratulated themselves, but it was subdued. Williamsport hadn't really put up a fight and they knew it.

It was a quiet bus trip back to Cranbrook. Nick didn't mind. He was glad they had won, but it was definitely his worst individual performance yet. His total scoring was one point, a free throw. He didn't want to dwell on it, so he cracked his algebra book to do a little homework. After a while, Dennis swayed down the aisle and plopped himself down next to him.

"What's going on?" he asked.

"Algebra," Nick responded, lifting his book a little.

"Tough game."

"How do you mean?" Nick asked, closing his book. He was glad Dennis had distracted him.

"I sure don't mean Williamsport was tough," Dennis said with a chuckle. "I mean for you."

"Yeah, I guess I didn't exactly tear it up."

"Everybody has an off day."

"Yeah, but it was weird. I just wasn't into the game, you know? I was actually bored."

"Bored? Wow. I just thought you were being your new, serious self."

Nick shrugged. Dennis was quiet for a minute. Then he spoke again.

"What's the deal with you, anyway?"

"No deal, just stopped fooling around. Everyone said I wasn't serious enough. So I changed, that's all."

"You changed, all right. I don't think I've seen you smile in a week. Being intense in practice is one thing, but you have to relax sometimes."

"I'll admit I haven't been having much fun, but practices have been good."

"Yeah, we've gotten a lot of work done. The minute you clammed up, everybody else got serious. Pockets was good today, huh?"

"Yeah, not bad at all."

"He was one guy who needed to take practice more seriously."

Nick was glad to unwind a little. Still, he couldn't understand what had gone wrong. Basketball had always been his favorite sport—he could never get enough of it. But Alden's next game was against St. Stephens, Tuesday afternoon, and Nick wasn't looking forward to it.

# 13

The third quarter was under way and the impossible was happening. St. Stephens, the team that had yet to win a game, was cruising along with a nine-point lead.

Alden had counted on St. Stephens to roll over and play dead. No such luck. The Panthers were being challenged on both ends of the floor. Surprised to find themselves in a tough basketball game, the Panthers became tentative, working too hard at setting up perfect plays. They stopped moving and forgot everything they had practiced, from boxing out to ball-handling. As they worried about making mistakes, they let St. Stephens control the tempo of the game.

After Alden committed two foolish turnovers in a row, Coach G. called time-out and gathered his team around him to settle them down. Now they were trailing 21–10. Not only was this game a disaster, but their title hopes were fading fast. They couldn't afford to lose this one.

It was the third time Coach had called time-out. He was exasperated.

"I've said it before, I'll say it again: Let's wake up out there," he barked. "I don't care if you lose, but you've got to give an effort. You're moving around like zombies. This is basketball. It's a *game*. I thought you guys liked to play."

Coach made a couple of lineup changes and called a give-and-go play for the next possession. Then he sent them back on the court. At the last second he called out to Nick.

"Wilkerson, come here."

Nick wondered what he wanted. Had he done something wrong? He jogged over. Coach G. looked both ways and then whispered: "Nick, the next time down the floor I want you to shoot one of those 'banzai' shots from half-court. With the yell."

Nick looked up with a start. He searched Coach's face.

Coach winked.

"Maybe it'll wake us up. Now get out there."

Nick ran on to the court. St. Stephens had the ball. They worked it around and scored on an eighteen-foot jumper: 23–10. Paul took the ball out of bounds and passed it in to Nick. Nick dribbled slowly up the court, thinking about what Coach had said. He could hardly believe it. He'd been going nuts trying to be more serious and now Coach *called* for a banzai bomb? He glanced at the sideline and saw Coach lift his eyebrows with a smile.

Nick smiled, too. In fact he almost laughed out loud. Coach G. really *did* want the banzai shot. Nick took a short low dribble and made a stutter step. The opposing guard was still waiting for him ten feet away. Nick shot with a yell.

"Banzai!"

The ball flew in a giant arc over the floor and every player from both sides stopped and watched in disbelief. A few of the Alden players glanced at Coach, expecting to see steam coming out his ears, but he was smiling and yelling "Banzai!" along with Nick.

The ball bounced hard against the backboard, missed the hoop completely, and shot down to the floor before anyone touched it. Pockets caught the ball on one hop, and found himself right underneath the hoop. He laid it up and in easily.

"I don't believe it," Justin said to Sam. "Coach must have *told him* to do that!"

"Ya gotta believe," Sam laughed.

"Are we giving up?" Justin asked.

"Just the opposite," said Sam. "We're starting over."

St. Stephens still led, 23–12, but Sam was right: everything had changed.

Both sides were abuzz over Nick's shot. They settled back into the game, but Coach G.'s odd strategy had worked. He had startled his team back to life.

Now they forgot all about the first three quarters, and forgot that they were losing to the worst team in the league. Alden was finally playing basketball. And win or lose, they were going to have fun.

Nick led the way, first scoring a fast-break hoop, and then making a three-point play when he was fouled while making a jumper from eight feet.

The Alden bench jumped to their feet.

"The bomber strikes!" Sam yelled.

"Do it up!" Justin called.

On defense Alden really came to life. They were hopping around like jumping beans, helping out, switching off. Whichever St. Stephens player had the ball also had a pair of Alden arms in his face. Nick's man drove in and Nick went for the steal, but missed as the St. Stephens guard made a dandy crossover dribble.

"Help!" Nick yelled.

"Go!" Pockets said, calling the switch. The guard head-faked, but Pockets stayed on his feet. Then he went up and Pockets went with him, swatting away the shot with ease. Kyle corraled the loose ball and led a two-on-one break with Dennis for an easy basket. Following the play, Nick and Pockets slapped hands.

"You faced that dude," Nick said with a smile.

"*Power* faced him," Pockets corrected.

Moving quickly, scoring on fast breaks when they could, and using the full-court press twice, Alden closed the gap. With just two minutes to go, Kyle hit a streaking Nick with an outlet pass. Nick easily outsprinted his man downcourt and laid in the tying basket. It was 30–30.

"Nice dish, Kyle!" called Paul, pointing at him.

"Let's do it."

Under Alden's full-court pressure, St. Stephens

finally did what they were supposed to do from the start—they collapsed. They missed shots. They made dumb fouls. They traveled. They had put up a great fight for thirty-eight minutes, but it only took two minutes for Alden to erase all memory of a St. Stephens lead. The final was Alden 37, St. Stephens 32.

Alden's title hopes were alive. The whole season had turned around on one shot. One ridiculous shot. One patented Nick Wilkerson mad bomber "banzai" special.

# 14

Pockets swung out of the low post with his back to the basket. Kevin rifled the ball in from the corner. Pockets caught it and faking left, went baseline for one dribble and made a sweet reverse lay-up.

As they ran back up court, Nick slapped Pockets on the back.

"Man, they're gonna change your name to Rockets! Where did you find that move?"

"Heck, this game is easy," Pockets joked.

The Alden Panthers were scrimmaging and Pockets *was* making the game of basketball look easy. Shooting, rebounding, passing, even dribbling. He was doing it all, leading the Skins to a 28–14 victory over the Shirts.

It was the end of the third practice in a row since the come-from-behind victory over St. Stephens. The team's mood was jubilant. They were putting their game together, having fun and working hard at the same time. With a record of seven wins against only three loses, Alden was now tied with Bradley for first place in the league standings. And Bradley was next on their schedule.

After practice, the day before the game, Coach asked Nick to stop by his office. Nick didn't know what was up.

"Hi, Nick, have a seat," Coach began. Nick put down his backpack and sat in a chair.

"This is no big deal, Nick, relax," Coach said. "You're not in trouble. I just felt I owed you an explanation. Or maybe it's not necessary. Do you know why you had to shoot that banzai shot?"

"Not really," Nick said. "I mean, I guess it was to make the team relax."

"That's it more or less. Basketball is funny. Some games you've got to bear down and push harder to get results, but basketball demands balance. You've got to be intense, but loose." Coach paused, then began again.

"As the team clown, you kept things loose. That's why I let you get away with so much fooling around. Sometimes, too much. But when you turned serious after the Lincoln game, the whole team lost its spirit." Coach was silent for a moment. "Well, I didn't mean to lecture your ear off, but I didn't want you to think I was playing mind games with you," he added.

"Thanks, Coach," Nick said. "It kinda makes more sense now."

"Good, take it easy. I'll see you tomorrow."

"Good night, Coach."

Nick picked up his bag and joined some of the guys who were waiting for rides in the gym lobby. They were figuring out the schedule and standings.

"Even if we lose to Bradley," Justin said, "we could still finish in a tie for first place."

"Oh, you don't think we can win, huh?" Sam asked with a smile.

"I didn't say that. I'm just looking at the mathematical possibilities. Bradley is 7–3 and so are we. If we lose, but then beat Lincoln we finish 8–4. Bradley would have to lose their last game for us to come in first."

"Who is Bradley playing?" Nick asked.

Justin flipped through the tattered notebook in which he kept all his notes and clippings about the Panthers.

"Here it is," he said, finding the list of schedules and scanning it. "Um, Williamsport."

Everyone groaned. Williamsport wasn't too good. Their record was 2–8 so far.

"Well, it looks like we have no choice but to beat Bradley ourselves," Nick declared.

"No kidding," Sam said.

"Yeah," Justin said. "If we beat Bradley, then we'll at least tie for the championship; and if we win both our last games, then we'll be league champions."

Mrs. Wilkerson's blue station wagon pulled into the semicircular drive and up to the curb. Sam was getting a ride with Nick, so they both climbed in.

"How was practice?" Mrs. Wilkerson asked.

"Totally wicked, great!" said Nick.

"Wow! Sounds it," Mrs. Wilkerson said with a laugh.

"You wouldn't believe it, Mom. We've gotten so much better."

"I believe, I believe."

Nick turned to Sam.

"Wasn't practice today great?"

"Definitely," Sam said.

"Everybody is getting better by the minute. Pockets is incredible."

"Practice has been more fun," Sam agreed. "And we've worked better as a team since you stopped being so angry."

"I wasn't exactly angry," Nick said. "I was just trying to be serious."

"Well, I'm glad you stopped. We need to work, but we need to stay loose, too. You know? A few laughs."

"Yeah, I know. I'm trying to stay intense more now. Guys like Pockets goof around too much if they don't keep their minds on practice."

"I guess," Sam said. "Whatever you're doing is working. I really think we can beat Bradley tomorrow."

Nick looked out the window.

"I know we can," he said.

The next day Nick was so eager to play the game that he was watching the clock in every class. By the time he got to his last class, biology, he could barely sit still. He was thinking about the game, when he heard Mr. Evans call his name.

"Nick, do you need to be excused?"

"Huh? No."

"I thought from the way you were squirming around perhaps you needed to go to the bathroom."

The class roared with laughter and Nick felt himself blush.

"Just try to sit still," Mr. Evans said.

Nick stopped jiggling his legs, but he still couldn't concentrate on class. When the final bell rang at last, he dashed for the locker room. All the Alden Panthers quickly dressed and boarded the bus for the trip to Bradley.

After arriving, they warmed up, noticing that a good group of parents and friends had made the trip to root for them. Coach G. gave them the final pep talk.

"Let's take it to them, now. We're going to run 'em into the ground. We're going to out-hustle 'em and out-muscle 'em. And"—he paused to smile—"we might just out-banzai them, too."

Everyone grinned.

"All right, let's go get 'em!"

The starters ran onto the floor and took their places. With a sharp, short whistle, the referee signaled the timekeeper to begin and tossed the jump ball up between Pockets and the Bradley center. Pockets got up to the ball first, but his tap was off. The ball was snatched and controlled by Bradley. Before the Alden defense could even set, a quick pass and a short jumper registered the game's first deuce. Bradley 2, Alden 0. The home crowd roared.

Kyle missed a jumper and Alden hustled back on defense. Bradley was more deliberate this time, passing the ball around outside, waiting for an opening. Patiently, the Alden players stuck with them. The ball went inside to Bradley's forward, but Nick read his shot perfectly and leapt to block the ball away. He was surprised to hear a whistle, but when he turned he saw the ref pointing at Pockets, not him. Foul. The Bradley man made one of two.

Alden missed and Bradley scored again. Now it was 5–0. The small pocket of Alden fans chanted "Dee-fense! Dee-fense!" Nick started to get anxious. They couldn't let this game get away. They had to turn it around now. Bradley had the ball, passing it around the outside. Nick took a chance. He lunged for a pass and tapped it away. Two steps ahead of his man, he corraled the loose ball and zipped downcourt for an uncontested lay-up. Bradley 5, Alden 2.

The game swung back and forth. Bradley held the lead until nearly the end of the second quarter, when

Alden turned on the heat. Nick sank two straight jump shots to bring them within one point of the lead.

In response Bradley slowed down their offense, carefully looking for any opening. But there was none, as the Alden cagers shifted smoothly, arms held high. Finally a desperate pass inside was deflected; Sam grabbed it. Dennis broke downcourt and Sam hit him on the fly with an overhand, quarterback pass. Dennis caught it, but the Bradley man, out of position, leapt for the ball. He knocked it away but committed the foul. Dennis made one of two shots; and the score was knotted at 15.

The Alden defense again held. They brought the ball back to their end of the court. Dennis set a pick and Nick stepped behind it perfectly, as the man guarding him bounced off Dennis and then awkwardly tried to get around. Free, Nick set himself and then jumped, cocking his wrist and then floating the ball up against the glass and in. The half ended, Alden 17, Bradley 15.

The home team was far from finished, though. The third quarter was all Bradley. They outplayed Alden, especially in the rebounding department. With two and three chances on each possession, Bradley recaptured their lead, and then padded it.

By the fourth quarter they rested on a six-point bulge.

Time was running out, but Alden wasn't quitting. They put the pressure on by getting tough on defense.

Bradley's guard had the ball just over half-court. Paul was guarding him and Alex came out to help press. The kid held his dribble and pivoted, looking for a pass. Nick's man, the other guard, was moving to the far side of the court, much too far away to get a pass. Nick had a crazy idea. He didn't think about it. He just did it. He stooped over and yelled at the guard with the ball: "Here! Here!"

It worked.

In that split second, the guy with the ball was so relieved to have help getting out of his jam that he didn't register who was helping. He threw the ball directly to Nick. Five dribbles and an easy lay-up later, Alden was back within four points, and Bradley was all shook up. Their coach called time.

On the Alden sideline, Coach G. rallied his players.

"They're on the run and let's keep it that way. We've got the sixth man going for us: momentum. Get out there and don't stop running!"

Alden stopped Bradley and scored again. Then

Bradley turned it over on a traveling violation. Then they fouled Pockets, who made one of two.

The Alden bench was clear as the players stood, yelling and cheering.

With less than two minutes to go, Alden trailed by a point. Finally, Bradley got back on the board, with a fifteen-foot jumper. Nick answered with a swish from eighteen feet.

"Do it, banzai man!" Sam yelled.

Then Bradley missed and committed a foul. Dennis sank one of two and the score was tied again at 44-all. The Alden bench went nuts. Everyone was calling out at once.

"Dee-fense. Dee-fense!"

"Arms up!"

"Stay with 'em!"

Bradley tried to work it around for the last shot, but their forward got nervous and put up a brick. Pockets snared the rebound and Alden had twenty-five seconds to score.

Nick brought the ball up. He already knew what he was going to try. Pockets had been playing the game of his life. Besides dominating the boards he had already scored nine points. Nick wanted to get it to him inside.

Bradley let him do it. Pockets anchored himself in

the low post, hands up, ready for the pass. Nick fired it to him high, and in one swift motion, Pockets latched onto the ball, turned toward the basket, and threw a head fake. The Bradley center went up, and as he came down again, Pockets went up. He angled it in off the board and Alden took the lead for good. Eight seconds and a desperation thirty-five-foot shot later, Alden had won.

The players rushed in from the sideline to mob Pockets.

On their way to the showers, Justin shook Nick's hand.

"Awesome game," Justin said.

"We are this close," Nick said, holding up his finger and thumb. "This close to the championship!"

"Are you kidding? We've got a lock," Justin said. "The worst we can do is be co-champions with Bradley if we lose to Lincoln."

"Unh, unh, pal," Nick said shaking his head. "We're not gonna be co-anything. We're going to win it all."

# 15

It had all come down to this. Alden versus Lincoln. The championship was on the line with just one minute and three seconds left in the game. One minute and three seconds left in the season.

It was Alden's last time-out. Nick stood catching his breath. His arms and legs were drained of all energy. Sweat gathered on his upper lip and he blew upward to spray it off. He pulled his glasses off for a moment, rubbing the bridge of his nose and then

pulled his sweaty jersey off his chest, flipping it back
and forth to cool down.

The score was Lincoln 31, Alden 29.

The bleachers in the Alden gym were full for the
first time all season, with fans of both the Panthers
and their crosstown rivals. Now they were all on
their feet. They had witnessed a battle, and as the
final minute ticked near, they were caught up in the
excitement. Every move on the court was followed
with intensity. Every misplay brought a round of
moans, every basket an explosion of cheers.

Neither team had been able to take a substantial
lead. The tension of the tight score had been building, adding pressure to an already explosive situation.

The Alden defense had been great. They were con-
stantly harassing the ball-handlers, forcing turnovers and misplays. They were an iron curtain
around the key, slamming down to stop any pene-
tration. Led by Pockets and Dennis, the rebounding
had been better than ever. They boxed out, got to
the ball first, and protected it. They were picture
perfect, like a page out of a playbook. Again and
again, Alden came down with the ball.

In more than one game during the season, Alden
had had their troubles putting the ball in the hoop,

but it was always poor shot selection, or sloppy passes, or just plain lazy play that had done them in. Today, it was good defense. They were moving the ball, hustling, picking and rolling, trying everything they knew, but Lincoln countered every move.

So they played even, with every point on the board hard-fought.

Now the only thing that mattered was the next one minute and three seconds.

"You guys have come too far to let down now," Coach said. "It's gut-check time and I know you can do it. You've got one minute to prove that you deserve that championship. Just do it."

The huddle broke up and the Alden five took the floor again for now or never time: Pockets O'Brien, Kyle Bushmiller, Dennis Clements, Paul Sacks, and Nick Wilkerson. The referee handed the ball to Nick on the sideline.

Nick took the ball and coolly spun it, finding a grip. He began scanning the court to find an open pass. The referee blew the whistle. Nick counted one-thousand-one, one-thousand-two, in his head. He had five seconds to make the pass. Nick pumped the ball once in Paul's direction, but his man was covering him too tightly. Just in time, Kyle cut away from his man. Nick hit him with the pass.

Paul and Nick crisscrossed and Kyle dumped it to Paul. He began to dribble, but the ball was knocked away. Luckily, he snatched it back quickly and bounced it to Nick. Fifty-eight seconds left.

Nick dribbled, walking slowly, surveying the floor. Out of the corner of his eye he saw Kyle and Pockets crowding inside. He picked up the pace of his dribble, moving in closer and turning his back to his defending guard. Dennis darted under the basket and skimmed by Kyle and Pockets, who had set up a double pick. He was free eight feet out and Nick found him with the ball. The pass caught the heel of Dennis's hand. He caught it, but it took a second for him to prepare his shot. By the time Dennis jumped, the man was there to block the shot, but he got a piece of Dennis's arm, too. The ref whistled the foul.

There were fifty-two seconds remaining, with the clock stopped. Dennis would shoot two. If he made them, the ball game would be tied.

While the other Panthers took their places around the key, Nick stood at half-court near the Lincoln guard.

"Let's do it, Dennis!" he yelled out. "You got it."

He clapped his hands. *Make them, Dennis,* he was thinking. *Make them, make them, make them.* Dennis bounced the ball once, twice. Nick had watched him shoot so many times he knew the rhythm of his bounces by heart. The first two bounces, the pause, the third bounce—and the shot. Nick held his breath.

Dennis missed.

For a moment, Nick clamped his jaw shut in frustration, but immediately he began to build his hopes again. They needed at least one point here. Dennis had to get this one.

"All right, let's get it, let's get it."

The first bounce, the second, the pause, the third bounce, and the shot. It was good and Lincoln's lead was cut to one slender point.

"Atsa my boy!" Nick said as he slapped Dennis on the back. Dennis smiled. Lincoln brought the ball up.

Nick went right to his man at the half-court line. He wasn't going to give him a free inch. Maybe he was too close. He was taking a chance of letting him get by. But he stuck like glue, razzing the man with a stream of chatter, along with his quick hands flashing wherever the ball was. He held the ball, then passed to the forward, deep in the corner.

Lincoln 31, Alden 30. Forty-four seconds to go.

The man faked going baseline, looked to the hoop,

but finally passed the ball back out. Nick's man got the ball and snapped it across to the other guard, who snapped it to the other forward. It was good passing, but it wasn't changing the score, and wherever the ball went, the Alden defense was there, too.

The pass went back to the guard, who went up for the shot. Paul's outstretched arm was in his face. The shot missed badly, hitting off the very front edge of the rim. It hit at such an extreme angle that it went over the hands of all the players jostling under the boards and was picked up by the other Lincoln guard. He was about to shoot it right up again, but Nick was on him, so he dribbled back, waiting to set up the offense.

Thirty-two seconds.

Nick stayed on him. He looked for an opening to try for the steal, but he didn't go for it. It was too dangerous. They were going to get one more chance down the floor. All they had to do was stop them here.

Lincoln was taking its time. Passing it around, they knew that all they had to do now was hold on. Around the outside it went, until Alden finally had to press. Pockets jumped out to help Kyle, pinning their forward to the sideline. The Lincoln forward found his man inside despite being surrounded by the long arms of Kyle and Pockets.

Fourteen seconds.

The Alden fans, the Alden bench, even Nick, from where he stood helpless, watched in dismay. The Lincoln center had the ball and an easy shot from six feet. He put it up.

Nick watched the ball, then he saw Dennis running in toward the hoop at full tilt and realized that he himself was standing there gaping. He also knew exactly what Dennis was thinking. Watching over his shoulder he took off in a sprint down court.

The shot missed.

Thirteen seconds.

Out of nowhere, Dennis snatched the rebound.

Twelve seconds.

Lincoln, who had settled into their stall tactics, was caught flat-footed.

Dennis took three quick dribbles to get out from under the baskets and then heaved the ball up the court.

Nick was wide open. He caught the pass just as the Lincoln pursuit reached him.

Ten seconds.

Nick drove for the hoop, but the defender took away the lane. Nick dribbled the ball once behind his back, picked up the dribble with his left hand, and went up for the left-handed lay-up.

It was good and a roar went up from the crowd. The Alden fans pounded the bleachers with their feet, making a thundering sound to match their yells.

Eight seconds. Alden 32, Lincoln 31.

Lincoln took the ball out of bounds and passed it in quickly. Too quickly. Dennis jumped at the pass, knocking it loose, and Paul dove to grab it. Four seconds.

Paul controlled the ball, but was flat on the ground. Lincoln leapt at him and succeeded in tying the ball up. There would be a jump ball, with one second left. It was over. The players on the Alden sideline were already celebrating the victory, their arms raised high in triumph.

The referee tossed up the jump ball and the Lincoln forward hit it. Before anyone could get it, the final buzzer sealed Alden's victory and championship.

The Panthers gathered in a mass, latecomers jumping on top.

"Hey, Coach G.," Nick yelled above the cheering, "can we cut down the nets as souvenirs?"

"You do and you pay for them," he answered, laughing.

113

"Well, at least let us pick you up and carry you."

"Oh no, you don't."

Nick looked around.

"Where's Justin? He's light enough for us to hold up."

Justin quickly took off for the locker room, but the players caught up with him, hoisted him high, and paraded around the court.

Things calmed down a little once they were inside the locker room. Coach congratulated each player individually. Soon he got to Nick.

"Well done, Banzai. You played a great game."

"Thanks, Coach."

"You've come a long way this season as a team player. Now just remember to mix it up: a little work, a little play, right?"

Nick smiled and nodded. As soon as Coach moved to the next row of lockers, Pockets, Dennis, Sam, and Justin gathered around.

"Well, guys, we did it," Dennis said. "We're the champs."

"Número uno," Justin said.

"What a season," Sam said.

"Greatest season ever," Pockets said.

"Until next year, that is," Nick said, and then he

took a can of soda out of his locker. "And now I propose a toast."

He shook up the can.

"To us!" he said as he opened it and sprayed them all. They laughed and ducked, but they all got wet. Nick poured what was left on his own head.